Words to Know Before You Read

donned

fancy

lumbered

pride

squeeze

stuff

trotted

twirled

wooly

© 2013 Rourke Educational Media

www.rourkeeducationalmedia.com

Edited by Precious McKenzie
Illustrated by Anita DuFalla
Art Direction and Page Layout by Renee Brady

Library of Congress PCN Data

Nobody's Watching / Kyla Steinkraus
ISBN 978-1-61810-195-2 (hard cover) (alk. paper)
ISBN 978-1-61810-328-4 (soft cover)
Library of Congress Control Number: 2012936796

Rourke Educational Media
Printed in the United States of America,
North Mankato, Minnesota

rourkeeducationalmedia.com

customerservice@rourkeeducationalmedia.com • PO Box 643328 Vero Beach, Florida 32964

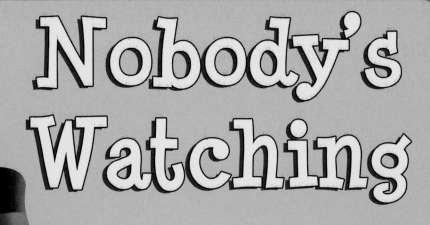

Nobody's Watching

By Kyla Steinkraus

Illustrated by Anita DuFalla

Ernest Elephant loved hats. He had a fancy hat for almost every day of the week.

On Mondays, Ernest wore a tall, black top hat.
On Tuesdays, he wore his dad's blue baseball cap.

On Wednesdays, Ernest put on a wooly, green beret. And on Thursdays, Ernest donned his fuchsia fedora.

Ernest was searching for a perfect hat for Friday.

7

One Monday at recess, Ernest was showing his friends how many balls he could stuff inside his tall, black top hat.

Just then, Priscilla Pony trotted by. Ernest gasped. On top of Priscilla's head was the most perfect red cowboy hat Ernest had ever seen!

9

"What a beautiful hat!" Ernest said.

Priscilla twirled the red cowboy hat in the air. "Thank you," she said. "It cost six dollars."

"I only have one dollar," Ernest sighed. "And my birthday is three whole weeks away."

Mike Monkey looked up from counting his lunch money. "I still like your old hats, Ernest."

Ernest slowly put his tall, black top hat back on his head. He wished it was a red cowboy hat instead.

After school, Ernest remembered he hadn't put the balls away at recess. He lumbered outside to the playground.

14

Five dollars sat on the picnic table next to the slide.

15

"That's enough for a red cowboy hat!" Ernest said.
Then he remembered the money belonged to Mike.

Nobody was watching. Nobody would know. Nobody would need the money as much as he did, he thought.

Then Ernest imagined just how hungry Mike would be because he wouldn't be able to buy lunch without his money.

"I would know I did it," Ernest said to himself. He knew he would feel terrible if someone took his money and he couldn't eat lunch.

The next day, Ernest gave Mike his lunch money. "Thank you, Ernest!" Mike squeezed his trunk in a big hug. Ernest felt happy.

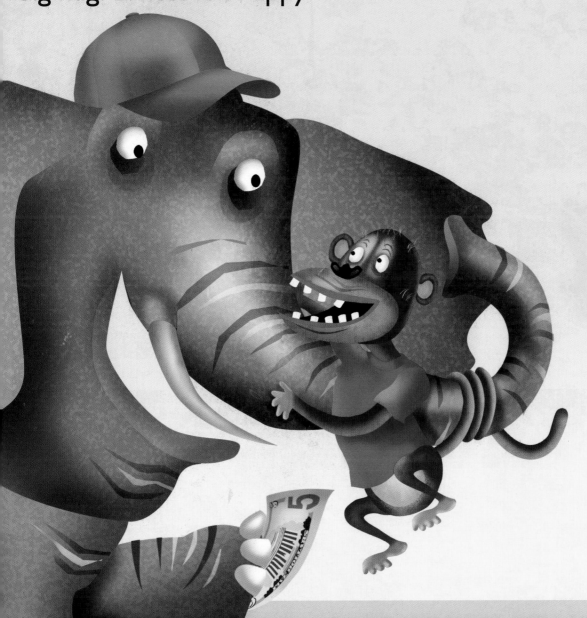

Ernest was even happier three weeks later when he opened his birthday present. It was a red cowboy hat just like Priscilla's!

Every Friday, Ernest wore his red cowboy hat with pride!

After Reading Activities

You and the Story...

What hat did Ernest wear on Mondays? On Wednesdays?

How much money did Ernest need to buy a red cowboy hat?

How do you think Mike would have felt if Ernest had taken the money?

What would you do if you found something that belonged to someone else?

Words You Know Now...

Look up each of the words below in a thesaurus. Write down two synonyms for each word. How is the meaning of the synonym different than the meaning of the original word?

donned	stuff
fancy	trotted
lumbered	twirled
pride	wooly
squeeze	

You Could...Perform a Play about Doing the Right Thing

Get together in a group with a few friends.

Create a story about a character who is tempted to do something wrong.
- Decide on characters.
- Decide what happens.
- Write it down.
- Make sure to include dialogue!

Make preparations.
- Make copies of your play for each person to practice.
- Decide who will play each role.
- Gather, make, and use props.
- Memorize your lines.

Practice together!

Find an audience and perform your play.

About the Author

Kyla Steinkraus lives in Tampa, Florida with her husband and two children. She really wants a red cowboy hat for herself, but she's glad Ernest has one.

Ask The Author!
www.rem4students.com

About the Illustrator

Acclaimed for its versatility in style, Anita DuFalla's work has appeared in many educational books, newspaper articles, and business advertisements and on numerous posters, book and magazine covers, and even giftwraps. Anita's passion for pattern is evident in both her artwork and her collection of 400 patterned tights. She lives in the Friendship neighborhood of Pittsburgh, Pennsylvania with her son, Lucas.

24